CONTENTS

3

4

5

6

7

*Dad

*Hello, girls!

8

10

12

13

14

16

18

20

22

23

33

43

48

49

69

ABOUT THE AUTHOR

With a love for all things pink and magical, Shauna J. Grant is a cartoonist who creates cuteness! Shauna is on a mission to add diversity to the comics community by creating stories that feature Black girls as the heroines of their own adventures, and her work has appeared in *Black Comix Returns, Noisemakers,* and *The Secret Loves of Geeks*. She enjoys spending her downtime daydreaming, reading Korean comics, and playing with her own magical dog, Sugarpaws. Shauna casts cuteness into the world via her comics from her home in New York City, the place she was born and raised.

Mimi and the
Cutie Catastrophe

Shauna J. Grant

An Imprint of
SCHOLASTIC

This book is dedicated to
my younger self and every child
following the magic inside their heart

Library of Congress Control Number: 2021937770

ISBN 978-1-338-76667-7 (hardcover)
ISBN 978-1-338-76666-0 (paperback)

10 9 8 7 6 5 4 3   22 23 24 25 26

Printed in China 62
First edition, July 2022

Edited by Megan Peace
Book design by Shivana Sookdeo
Creative Director: Phil Falco
Publisher: David Saylor